Christmas with Man – A Short, Steamy Instalove Mountain Man Holiday Romance

Mountain Men of Charming Falls

By Ann Ric

Copyright 2023 Ann Ric, SR

All rights reserved; no part of this publication may be reproduced or transmitted by any means, electronic, mechanical, photocopying or otherwise, without the prior written permission of the publisher.

This book is a work of fiction and created entirely and solely by the author's own imagination. The names, characters, places, and incidents are products of the writer's imagination or have been used fictitiously. Any resemblance to persons, living or dead, is entirely coincidental.

Books by Ann Ric

Mountain Men of Charming Falls

Rescued by the Mountain Man (Evie & Jake)
Claimed by the Mountain Man (Candi & Erik)
Stranded with the Mountain Man (Lilly & Alex)
Christmas with the Mountain Man (Harmony & Chase)

Magic Protector Reverse Harem Trilogy

Magic Protector – A Steamy Paranormal Reverse Harem Romance (Book 1)
Magic Bound – A Steamy Paranormal Reverse Harem Romance (Book 2)
Magic Promise – A Steamy Paranormal Reverse Harem Romance (Book 3)

Christmas with the Mountain Man

After her now-ex broke off with her last Christmas, Harmony decided to never marry or celebrate the holidays...but her godmother had other plans. Harmony finds herself in Charming Falls to put up the Christmas tree in her godmother's *Happily Ever After* log cabin while she's away. But she soon runs into unexpected trouble in the form of a strikingly gorgeous mountain man.

Ex-military mountain man Chase wasn't looking for love, until love came to his door...his mother's friend asked him to put up the Christmas tree in her log cabin. But he wasn't expecting an intruder; a beautiful curvy woman…

***

Welcome to ***Mountain Men of Charming Falls***, the spicy instalove series based on a picturesque small mountain town by a lake that brings you closer to nature. A tranquil scenic escape from the busy city where residents in the cozy close-knit community look out for each other. Let the cool mountain breeze, clear night skies, beautiful romantic sunsets, and the fresh pine scents that fill the air bring you serene relaxation. Known for its camping sites, rustic cabin retreats, hiking trails, ski slopes, and yes, semi-recluse hot and sexy ex-military mountain men who live by the honor code: respect, loyalty, selfless service, integrity and courage in everything they do. Charming Falls is the perfect place to fall in love.

Chapter 1 - Harmony

Harmony rubbed her arms, shivering as she stood outside her godmother's empty log cabin in Charming Falls. She thought she had the right key for the front door but she was obviously wrong.

The snow fell hard outside. She couldn't believe it was the eve before Christmas. According to some statistics, as many as twenty-eight percent of the population were either single or lived alone.

And this was more pronounced during festive holiday times like Christmas that emphasized togetherness and family time.

Right now, Harmony should be strolling through the *Charming Falls Christmas Market* with the man of her dreams enjoying the lights, music and festive decorations. Instead, she'd become a statistic: single and alone over the holidays.

Well, at least she had her health. That was a good thing, right? Her godmother had always told her to count her blessings, not her troubles. And she had an adorable godmother who always looked out for her. Someone whom she would do *anything* for.

She'd promised to help her ailing godmother out by going to her log cabin in the small mountain town and turning on the tree lights. It was some sort of ritual her godmother did every year since her godfather passed. Her godparents had apparently spent many happy holidays there in the mountains at their cozy cabin hideaway. Her godmother was too ill to make it this year.

She knew that Harmony no longer celebrated the holidays—not since that horrible Christmas Eve last year when her now ex-boyfriend broke off with her by text message when he'd found someone new. She blinked back tears, trying to sweep that memory out of her head.

Harmony had always been a planner. Everything had to be planned in her life. She was going to get her advanced degree in Social Work. Then get into a decent job in the community that made a difference in people's lives. Then get married and have two point four children—all before turning thirty. But that probably wasn't going to happen now. Her ex had other plans.

He'd told her she wasn't the right fit for his image. He was an exec in sports management. He'd told her she was way too heavy for him and he wanted someone who looked good beside him at company events.

She was not going to give her cheating ex any more room in her head. He didn't deserve it.

Her friends were with their own families now. Harmony didn't have any close family now.

She had accepted that she would be on her own; alone—for now.

And Christmas was a holiday she no longer celebrated. Yes, it was hard on the lonely. That's why being up there in the mountains in the cabin while everyone else celebrated with their loved ones—would suit her fine. She was very happy for them but she'd given up on love herself. Maybe it wasn't for everyone, she thought.

Harmony let out a puff of air as she walked back to her car. She didn't know what she was going to do now that she was locked out of the cabin. She'd planned to stay inside where it would be nice and warm.

Why was it that her plans always went up in smoke? Maybe she shouldn't plan for anything.

And speaking of smoke. Maryanne, her godmother had told her that her neighbor, Chase, had already put firewood by the fireplace. She could use that warmth from the fire right now.

Chase.

She hadn't seen that gorgeous recluse in so long.

They'd gone to high school together but she never got close to him. He was a senior and she was a junior. He mostly kept to himself. And thinking back now—who could blame him?

He was a strange one. He'd helped her out once, when some guys started troubling her because of her weight. Making fun of her in the hallways between classes. Well, he'd stood up for her then.

But…

He never spoke to her since.

And even after she'd thanked him, he just kept away. He wasn't much for words. But she'd always admired him from afar back then.

Still, she heard he'd moved to the mountains after his honorable discharge from the army and worked on building homes in the area. Something like that.

Charming Falls was a cozy small mountain town. Small talk got around. It was hard not to know what most people were up to. Someone knew somebody. She'd heard that a few guys moved up to the mountains, ex- military soldiers. There were many log cabins there.

She couldn't imagine living there year round where it was so cold—even in the summer. But especially now, so close to winter.

Harmony walked around the cabin to see if there was another door.

Nope. No other door.

She then pulled out her cell phone.

"Of course there would be no cell service around here. Great," she whispered to herself as a puff of visible air escaped her quivering lips again.

Man, it was cold out there.

How could Chase live out here? she thought to herself.

She'd always wondered what her grumpy fellow high schooler was up to.

Speaking of grumpy, she thought she heard a low growling sound.

"Oh, no. Please don't be what I think it is." Her heart started to beat hard and loud in her chest. She wondered if the animal, whatever it was, could hear her pounding heart.

She had to get back into her car.

She walked over to her car, hugging herself but stopped cold.

Her body tensed.

It was freezing outside but right now heat burned through her cheeks.

She was not going to get anywhere near her car now.

The grizzly bear, standing at the driver's side door, probably wasn't going to let her.

Chapter 2 - Chase

Chase made his way to Ms. Maryanne's cabin. Every year the nice old lady wanted him to turn on the Christmas tree lights to her cabin. She used to live there with her husband before he passed away. She'd told him it was a good luck ritual they did every year and she'd promised her husband that she'd continue that holiday tradition.

He was happy for her that she'd found the love of her life and even after he died, she still held a candle to him or a lit Christmas tree. But Chase didn't believe in love. Not anymore anyway.

He rubbed the stubble on his chin. The wind was brisk outside. The town was expecting another ten centimeters of snow. It was going to be a cold one tonight.

He'd read over the instructions again on his phone just before getting into his truck. She wanted him to stay at the cabin and stand in front of the lit tree so that she could see it from her retirement home. Then take a snapshot and send a picture to her WhatsApp.

There was a mistletoe at the cabin entrance.

It was called the *Happily Ever After Cabin* and the mistletoe was supposed to bring some form of good luck.

Well, his eccentric neighbor really had a sense of humor, he thought to himself.

They were such a happy couple from what he remembered. He was glad to be able to help them out over the years doing things for them. Helping them get set up for winter and chopping wood for her husband when he got too old to do it. Her husband, like Chase, had served in the military. He was honored to help a fellow vet out.

There was something peaceful about being up in the mountains, away from everyone.

That's just the way Chase liked it.

Spending Christmas alone.

Especially since that heartbreaking Christmas in his past. He just didn't believe in all that love stuff or fuzzy feeling. Whatever it was called.

He turned on the ignition and made his way over to Maryanne's cabin, hoping the cell phone service would stay on.

The cellular connection wasn't reliable around there. It got spotty at times.

Just then a call came in.

"Hey, Chase. You coming to the bar in town?" his friend asked.

His army buddies, usually got together for a drink at the Charming Falls Cozy Bar and Grill, especially around the holidays.

"Depends," he said. "Remember, Ms. Maryanne?"

"Oh, yeah, right. She and her husband were really something. She okay?"

"Yeah, she just wants me to set up her tree and send her a picture."

"Oh, right. That annual ritual. Man, that's really nice of you. You really need to get a life though."

He bristled. "I don't think so. My life's out here in the mountains."

"Don't you get lonely?"

He did. But he wasn't going to admit it. It wasn't worth being in a relationship. In fact, it had been over a year since he'd been with a woman. He found it hard to open up on two occasions. Day and night. And that was fine by him.

Love could be painful—especially when it got messed up.

He wasn't going to ever do that again.

Not to mention Chase didn't do casual sex. He wanted to be with someone that he was committed to. He knew that made him different from a lot of other guys—but Chase had always been different.

He was his own man. On the outside, he was a big guy with tats. That's probably all people saw of him. They didn't know the real Chase. And he would keep it that way.

Chapter 3 - Harmony

Harmony's heart raced in her chest.

Was she going to die out there in the mountains?

What was she going to do now?

Luckily, the bear wasn't paying her any mind.

Soon, it wondered away.

She sucked in a deep breath then breathed out a sigh of relief.

"That was close." She swallowed hard.

But she wasn't out of the woods yet, so to speak. And she knew that.

She knew the bear could come back any time. Being outside in the mountains was no place for a woman.

What was she going to do?

She glanced around to make sure there were no other wild animals around then she quickly made her way to her car.

She then turned on the engine when…

A horrible sound erupted. And smoke billowed from the front of the car.

"Oh, no. Oh, no, no, no. Not this. Not now."

She turned off the engine and got outside.

It was just what she thought.

Her car had died.

"Great, my phone service is dead. My car is dead. And so will I be, if I don't get inside soon."

What was she going to do?

What if the bear came back?

She had nowhere to hide.

She shivered and tried hard to keep warm but it was no use. She was probably going to die out there in the cold. And worse! She could get attacked by a bear or a wolf.

Oh, no.

Suddenly, she felt dizzy and sat down on the porch of the cabin. She didn't get a chance to eat anything that morning. Was she getting hypothermic?

Then…

It all went dark.

***

Harmony didn't know how long she had been out. But when she woke up, she was inside the cabin on the couch with a warm blanket over her.

The scent of baked chicken and potatoes wafted to her nostrils.

She saw the back of a tall man at the stove making some dinner. He had broad shoulders and wore a lumber jacket.

How on earth did she get into the cabin? Who was he? Was he going to hurt her? But then again, it didn't look like it.

As if sensing something, he turned around.

And her jaw fell wide open.

It was Chase.

And he looked more stunning than she'd ever remembered. He was tall, strikingly handsome with the most beautiful face she'd ever seen on a man. But his expression was that of concern mixed with confusion.

"Are you okay, Harmony?" he asked, pointedly.

"Um…yes. Chase. What are you doing here? How did I get in here?"

His expression was blank. He always had an unreadable expression on his face. He was never much for communicating from what she'd remembered. He wasn't very sociable. Though he was always helpful. Just as he'd helped her out in the past when they were in high school.

"You almost froze to death out there," he said. "I'm making you something to eat. You like chicken, right?" he asked, as if nothing out of the ordinary.

"Oh, my goodness. You… you saved my life, Chase. I…I could have died out there. Thank you so much."

"It was nothing." He went back to turning the chicken in the oven then closing the oven door. "Dinner should be ready soon."

But he still didn't answer the question of what he was doing there.

"Are you kidding me? I could have died out there. It *was* something. I really appreciate it."

He didn't say anything.

"Mmm, that smells delicious. I had no idea you could cook."

"Thanks," he said, quietly.

"What are you doing here in Maryanne's cabin?" she asked, hoping to not sound ungrateful.

Did he break into the cabin? Where did he get the food? Did he know she was going to be there?

"She asked me to set up the Christmas tree lights for her to see. It's a tradition."

She laughed, heartily. "She told me the same thing. I wonder if she forgot she already asked me to do that. Not that I'm

19

complaining, of course." Her voice was cheerful.

"Of course."

"So how do you like living out here?"

"It's good," he said. "I have my own business, supplying lumber and helping to build homes."

"That is so amazing!"

"Thanks. The people I work with and work for are amazing. I wanted to give back to the community and spend time up on the mountains after serving. It's a great honor to be here."

"I can imagine," she said, admiringly.

She'd always loved the feel of the town whenever she visited. It was so cozy and everyone looked out for each other there. Unlike her the city. People were nice to each other there. And Charming Falls could describe the people as well as the town. There were so many events and festivals in Charming Falls, not to mention the great ski slopes and hiking trails. It was like a paradise there. Of course, like Chase, she grew up in the next town from Charming Falls. She didn't know anyone else there except her godmother—and now Chase. She never thought about living there before. But maybe she should think about it. She could get to see more of Chase.

The snow fell harder outside as the wind howled. She was so grateful to be indoors right now. And with a gorgeous old school friend. Or old school acquaintance. Someone she'd always admired from afar but was too afraid to get too close. Especially since he wasn't very sociable.

He turned off the oven and took out some plates from the cupboard. He sure knew his away around the kitchen. He knew where everything was. She knew Maryanne had asked him to make sure that firewood would be set up in the fireplace but she never figured he'd also had a tour of the place.

She noticed a thermometer on the counter and Chase told her he'd taken her temperature when he'd brought her in from the cold, to make sure she was okay and checked her vital signs. He'd also checked her over again to make sure she didn't have frost bite. Her hero. She was so grateful he'd seen her when he did.

She'd never been this close to Chase before. Her body responded to his touch, surprising her. Her nipples tightened underneath her top and she felt a sweet sensation between her legs at his nearness.

She caught a whiff of his delicious cologne. And she couldn't help but notice his strong muscles and his physique. He was fit. He'd always taken great care of his body from what she remembered. He used to play all the sports at school and work out at the gym.

***

An hour later, they sat in silence at the small oak dinner table in the cabin.

"You are such an amazing cook," she said.

"Thanks," he said, his tone was soft and deep.

He probably thought she was an idiot for being out there in the cold like that. How embarrassing. He didn't even ask her what she was doing out there.

"Thank you for taking care of me," she said, after they'd finished eating.

"I'm glad you're all right," he said. His sexy gaze caught hers for a moment and there was something sweet in his eyes but then he looked down at his plate. Was he blushing?

She knew he wasn't much of a communicator back in high school when he'd rescued her and even now. And the rumor was that he was shy around girls. But, oh, he was the hottest guy in high school. All the girls drooled over him. Some thought he was aloof.

But deep inside he was a sweetheart. Unlike the other guys she'd met who tried to impress her with their fake charm, but Chase was the real deal. And for some reason, she was drawn to him, attracted to him. But why was he keeping his distance?

She wondered if he was seeing anyone.

Maybe that was it. Maybe he was involved with someone else.

He got up to do the dishes.

"I'll do them."

"You don't have to," he said, gently.

Warmth slid inside her of his sweet sentiment. "I want to," she said, playfully. "It's my godmother's house. Let's do them together."

He had done most of the work but she grabbed a dish from the rack to dry, even though he'd insisted he would do all the work.

When their fingers brushed while putting away the dishes, there was a spark between them. Butterflies fluttered about in her belly.

She wondered what would happen now.

Chapter 4 - Chase

Chase had to keep his feelings in check. But that wasn't easy around lovely Harmony. He couldn't believe he was seeing her again after all this time. He'd always had a crush on her in high school.

He liked everything about her. She was always humble and smart and always had her nose in a book. She didn't run around or get into trouble like some of the other students in the school.

But he'd always been shy around girls he liked. And he liked her a lot. He always had. In fact, he didn't want anything to spoil his casual friendship with her. He'd thought about asking her out once but then he stopped himself. He was a man that kept mostly to himself. And some girls didn't like that. He liked to spend a lot of time alone—meditating. It wasn't anything personal but then his ex had left him because of it. He figured he'd be a loner and that was fine by him. Especially after he'd left the military. He didn't do emotions well. Ordinarily, he didn't like to open up to or get too close to anyone because he was afraid of having his heart broken—he was afraid of losing them.

Or maybe it was because he hadn't found the right girl. Until now…

Why did his mind go there? Why did he feel so different around Harmony?

Was Harmony seeing someone? He though he heard Ms. Maryanne say something about her having a boyfriend last year.

"Shouldn't you be with your boyfriend at Christmas?" He hoped he didn't sound rude by blurting it out like that. Again, conversational skills weren't his thing—unfortunately.

"We broke up." Her cheeks colored.

Chase felt his heart crush in his chest for her. "Sorry to hear that. What happened?"

"Well, he wasn't faithful. I stopped believing in happily ever after." She grinned. "Yes, I know the name of this cabin is Happily Ever After."

He grinned back.

"Anyway," she continued. "I no longer celebrate the holidays because it feels so painful when you're alone."

"Sorry to hear that. And you're right. It can be lonely for those who live alone."

"Tell me about it. People always judge the single people over the holidays. Like we don't' have it hard enough."

He grinned. "What about your family?" Chase hoped he wasn't probing much but something about Harmony made him feel good about talking. This was probably the most talking he'd ever done. He wasn't a man of many words.

"They've passed on. And my ex was supposed to be my family. But I realize we weren't mean to be. I never did feel the sparks. And neither did he. I think we just didn't want to hit thirty and still be single. But I realize now, we never had any chemistry. Or anything in common. And I wasn't his type."

"What makes you say that?"

"I wasn't model-friendly enough for his crowd. He kept telling me to lose weight or change my hair."

His brows furrowed. "You are amazing just the way you are. You're so beautiful," he said and he meant ever word of that.

Her cheeks colored.

"Thanks. My ex never told me that."

"He's an idiot."

She burst out laughing. The sound of her laughter sounded like her name, harmonious. Her energy was light. It drew him in like a magnet. Her beauty captivated him. He could feel his hard-on in his pants and hoped she wouldn't notice.

She was everything his ex was not. Charming, delightful, curvy, sexy and a darling to be around. This was the most he'd ever talked with anyone in a long time.

"You have everything I desire in a woman," he blurted out. "Curves in all the right places. You're friendly, and caring, looking out for your godmother—especially on Christmas Eve in the middle of a storm."

She blushed. "But not every man thinks that way. They think there's too much of me, I guess."

"You're perfect. You're enough. You don't deserve your ex. He's missing out on a lot. I mean that."

He could see the appreciation on her face and those lips, oh, man, he had to keep his eyes away from her sweet shapely lips that looked so kissable. The image of him pressing his lips over hers slid into his mind.

"Thanks," she said, softly.

He couldn't believe anyone would treat her that way. He'd always been protective of her.

He felt his erection straining. He had to divert his attention away from her before she noticed.

"Well, let's get this tree decorated."

She looked surprised and he hoped he didn't offend her. He wanted to listen to her speak more about her life but he also wanted to hide his attraction to her.

Besides, they had to get the tradition going for Maryanne's sake.

"Isn't it special?" she said, about the tree.

"Sure is."

"It's amazing Maryanne and her husband had such a long happy relationship."

"They were meant for each other." He looked into her eyes then tore his gaze away.

He didn't know what he wanted right now. But he wanted Harmony. He just didn't want to scare her away.

Chapter 5 - Harmony

Harmony's heart fluttered in her chest. Being near Chase made her heart giddy with excitement and there they were. Alone. In a cabin named the *Happily Ever After Cabin* on Christmas Eve. Two old friends who cared about each other but never got too close.

She wondered what his lips would feel like.

She loved the way his eyes roamed with admiration over her curves. He looked at her in a way her ex never did. Chase appreciated her for who she was. Her heart fluttered with delight over the feeling he gave her. She felt so good in his presence. She felt as if she were enough—more than enough.

Was it fate that brought them together tonight?

Or was it their mutual delightfully scheming godmother who was playing a little sneaky matchmaking.

She wondered now. Her godmother never told her she'd be spending the night at the cabin with a sexy roommate. Her old school friend.

Maryanne had told her to take the guest room that came with its own ensuite bathroom including a shower. She would have to take a shower in the guest room soon.

She wondered if Chase would be staying in the other guest room. Since the spacious cozy cabin had so many rooms.

Deep down, she couldn't believe she hoped they'd share the same room.

Harmony thought she'd spend Christmas alone—again. But this may turn out to the most heartwarming Christmas ever!

Perhaps, her godmother knew they'd hit it off.

She knew them both separately, after all.

They spent the next two hours playfully decorating the tree while listening to Christmas music on the old CD player in the cabin. Maryanne had left it there for anyone to listen to while decorating.

It was a great idea. It lifted their mood and certainly put her in the Christmas spirit. The first in a long while. Funny, she never felt this way last year. Maybe because she was alone. She wasn't in the company of a gorgeous and kind mountain man like Chase.

That's what made the difference.

The holiday spirit wasn't the same without someone you cared about and someone that cared about you.

People made the holidays. Not things.

Surrounded by those you cherished made it all worth it. It had been so long since she'd had that. She never thought she'd get into the holiday mood again after her disastrous previous relationship that got cancelled right before Christmas. And after losing her family so many years ago.

After they finished decorating the tree. Chase took a picture of it for Maryanne and sent it.

"This will make Maryanne happy," he said.

"You are amazing for doing that," she said.

"She was like a mother to me," he said. "And you're nice to do that for her too. I'm sure she really appreciates you looking after her cabin for her—especially around this time of the year."

Harmony smiled; a warm feeling slid inside her being near Chase.

"You never told me about your…um…plans…" she said, wanting to find out if he had a girlfriend that he left behind somewhere.

"I'm alone. I don't really speak to anyone much."

"You spoke to me this evening," she smiled warmly.

"I know. I realized my ex and I didn't have much in common and that's why we probably didn't communicate much. This is the most I've spoken in a long while. I'm not really much for conversations."

"Are you kidding me," she smiled warmly. "You made me feel so good opening up to you. You are a great conversationalist."

"Thanks. Sometimes I just say what's on my mind and it upsets people."

"I like the way you are, Chase. I wish my ex had told me what was on his mind and it would have saved me a lot of heartache. You're honest and sincere and you mean well. That's noble of you."

She saw something in his eyes, an intense heat of desire. And she connected to him instantly. A magical feeling lingered in the air between them. She felt a pull towards his magnetic charm and stunningly sexy body.

Just then, the mistletoe he'd hung earlier was hanging over them.

Oh, god. She wanted him.

Did he feel the same way about her?

Would he kiss her now?

She wondered if he was going to kiss her.

"Do you think my fairy godmother planned this?"

He grinned, a sexy dimple appeared on one of his cheeks. God, he was adorable.

"I wouldn't put it past her. She's a sweetheart. And a matchmaker from what I've been told."

"Well, it is the *Happily Ever After Cabin*," she cooed.

She leaned up to him and he leaned down to her.

Their lips brushed gently against each other and he kissed her sweetly.

Man, his lips were so soft and sweet. She'd never been kissed like that before. Ever.

"What are we doing?" she breathed, enjoying every moment.

"Celebrating Christmas."

She thought she'd never do that again. But all of a sudden, she wanted him more than anything.

She kissed him again. And he kissed her back hungrily.

He then stopped and looked so admiringly into her eyes. "You're the most beautiful woman I've ever laid eyes on. And since we're being open tonight. I wanted you to know."

"Oh, Chase. I feel the same way about you. I mean, you're the sexiest man I've ever met. Distant, though…" she added, playfully.

"I'm sorry. I was never good at these things. Especially when I saw a girl I really liked."

"You really liked me in high school."

"I couldn't stop thinking about you. You're so amazing in every way. Smart, beautiful. Kind."

She kissed him again. "I want you," she breathed, waves of desire rolling through her.

It had been over a year since she'd been intimate. Way too long. And she wanted this more than anything. She wanted to celebrate being alive, especially after what happened tonight. He saved her life.

She could feel the hard erection in his pants as he leaned into her. She knew he wanted her too.

Being spontaneous was so unlike her. She always used to take her time to spend more time with a man first. But then again, she'd known Chase since high school. And she thought she knew her ex…and he ended up breaking her heart in the worst way. So…

Just then a light feeling slid inside her.

She wanted Chase more than anything. Her feelings for him from high school had been rekindled on this magical night. Especially after he'd just save her life. Yet again.

"You know what," she murmured.

"Hmm," he said.

"I'm usually always a planner. Everything has to be planned out in my life. Even my dates."

"Is that so," he murmured, his lips curved slightly into an amused grin.

God, he looked so charming when he did that.

They were inches from each other and the scent of his sweet cologne wafted to her nostrils.

He was irresistible in every way.

"Yes. And look where it's gotten me. Jilted over the Christmas last year. So…" she said. "Maybe it's time to do things differently for a change." She gave him a naughty grin.

"I'm so sorry you went through all that. You deserve to be treated like a queen. I want to do that. I've admired you for so long," he groaned as he pressed his lips to hers again.

Sparks flew inside her.

She'd never done this before. Being so close to a man that she wasn't in a long term relationship with—not that she had much experience.

Maybe she should try something different for tonight with a guy she'd known so long. A guy that really cared about her as much as she really cared about him.

"I need a shower," she breathed heavily.

"Same here. Want to shower together?" he moaned in a low sexy deep voice.

Her nipples hardened at the thought. Her pussy throbbed with want. She was so turned on by his deep, sexy aroused voice.

Were they going to be spontaneous?

Maybe she should do the opposite of what she'd ever done. Live in the moment. And right now, desire swept through her body for her old high school friend.

"Please," she begged, as they hungrily kissed and made it to the shower room.

Before long, they had stripped off each other's clothes and were in the shower.

He. Was. Huge!

His hard cock was big. His abs were muscular. And his skin was so perfect with all those tattoos decorating his shoulders.

Were they really going to be intimate tonight?

Chapter 6 - Harmony

Moments later, as they both stood under the warm flowing water of the shower in the guest room's ensuite bathroom. Chase grabbed a soft sponge and added an aromatic rose scent body wash.

"Let's make this fun," he said, seductively.

"Never had a dual shower before," she cooed. She wanted to add, especially with a hot and sexy mountain man with a killer body.

"First time for everything." A sweet grin curved his sexy soft lips.

"I want to pleasure you in all the ways you deserve, Harmony." She loved the say he said that. She loved the sound of his voice. She loved the look in his eyes when his ocean blue eyes slid down the curves of her body.

His erection was huge in response.

"Oh god, you turn me on," he groaned as they both lathered up and he gave her a nice massage sliding his fingers over every inch of her body starting with a sensuous back rub as the bubbly white foamy sudds slid down her skin.

He then massaged her erotically as they showered together. Starting with circling her breasts tenderly then his fingers slid over her hard nipples and her breath quickened; she gasped with delight. She loved this feel.

The pleasure slid through her body at his soft touch as he intermittently pressed soft passionate kisses to her naked skin.

He took his time.

Her ex had never taken his time before. Not that they'd done it in the shower. In fact, she'd only had one boyfriend before and they were hardly intimate.

But this? This felt different. So special. So romantic. Erotic. Elevating.

He inhaled her scent from behind as he kissed her neck and told her how beautiful she was and how he loved every inch of her.

His hands slid down her wet curves. Soon she returned the favor and washed his skin, arousal sweeping through her at the silky feel of his muscular skin. He was perfect. Every inch of him was perfect.

"This is hard," she breathed.

A puzzled expression slid across his gorgeous face. "I can't do this without being so turned on," she grinned sheepishly..

Her eyes darted to his huge cock. She wanted him now and then. Their skins were clean and the soap had vanished as warm water splashed over their naked bodies in the shower.

"Oh, Harmony, I love you. I want you so badly. I've always wanted you. I want to be inside you now," he groaned with pleasure.

"I…I love you too, Chase," she said, breathless; her voice a soft aroused whisper.

He sucked on her skin and her inner thighs pulsed hard and fast. Just the feel of his lips on hers made her hot all over.

She thought she was having a warm shower but there was nothing warm there. This was hot. Too hot to handle and she loved it. She wanted more of Chase.

She was soaking wet between her legs and she knew it had little to do with the water flowing over their naked skins. She wanted Chase now.

"I brought a condom," he groaned between hot kisses.

"Please, I…I need you," she said, breathing heavily. She felt relieved he was prepared.

He was back in the shower with her in no time and placed the condom pack at the edge of the tub. Hunger filled his eyes as he continued to make out with her in the shower, caressing every inch of her body. His fingers slid into her folds from behind as she leaned back into him, enjoying the feel of his cock against her back. Her body anticipating more of him. She liked that he was taking his time. She savored his touch, his sweet caresses.

"You like that, beautiful," he said.

She groaned with pleasure in response.

He then turned her around and lowered himself to her pussy, leaning her back so she could support herself against the wall of the shower stall, her knees slightly bent, her legs spread for him. He then sucked and teased her wet folds and it felt so amazing between her legs. His tongue strokes were rhythmic and pleasurable as desire flood through her veins.

Soon, she felt the buildup of orgasm. He stopped as she breathed hard, begging for more.

"Not yet, baby. Don't come yet. I want my dick inside you when you come."

A grin of approval touched her lips. She liked the sound of that. The buildup was perfect for the reward of having all of Chase fill her.

She then leaned down and stroked his cock as he groaned, breathing hard. She grabbed his firm ass as she took his dick in between her lips, sucking back and forth. He moaned and groaned with pleasure. She loved the sound coming from his throat as she pleased him. He tasted so good, like a trace of fresh soap. Just as he was on the brink. He guided her up and they brushed their lips against each other's, kissing hungrily, tasting each other's sex on their lips. He leaned her against the marble shower wall. Then he slid on his condom after opening the packet. Eyeing her with admiration.

"I've always wanted you, Harmony. You have no idea how much I've also admired you and treasured you."

"Same here," she breathed, kissing him hungrily, not wanting him to stop.

"You want this now?"

"Yes, please. I…I want you now. I…can't…wait." Her pussy pulsed hard wanting him inside her now. Her body was on fire for him.

Before long he guided his hard cock into her small opening and she gasped with delight as he slowly rocked back and forth sliding in and out of her, completely out and then back in again. She loved the way his cock filled her pussy, so tightly. He felt so good.

"Oh, Chase. I…want you now…" She moaned as Chase sucked on her neck, rhythmically while he moved in and out of her, his hands up on the wall steadying her between him while she leaned back. Their wet skins slapping against each other. He thrust back and forth, deeper and faster and faster until, she came with an explosive orgasm sending waves of pleasure ricocheting through her body.

Wow.

That was so fucking amazing.

Her body convulsed with orgasmic pleasure as Chase moved his arms around her and hugged her firmly. His body soon spasmed with orgasmic release as he came inside her. Breathing hard and heavy, both grinning with sated pleasure, they collapsed into each other's arms after they came. He pressed sweet kisses to her lips and then she hungrily kissed him back.

That. Was. Amazing.

So, she'd made mad passionate love in the shower to her hot mountain man friend. But would that be it? Would she ever get a chance to be with Chase again? The thought of never experiencing this passion with Chase again made her legs feel weak.

***

The next morning, she woke up feeling surreal. She wanted more of Chase. She was so appreciative of the time they'd spent together.

It had been magical. But what would happen next? She loved being around him. She loved how he made her feel. She loved how she felt with him. Around him.

The delicious scent of breakfast wafted to her nostrils. No one had ever made her breakfast before. Not counting going to a restaurant, of course.

Breakfast was already set on the table. The Christmas tree lights sparkled on the tree in the cabin. She could feel the positive energy in the air.

"Merry Christmas," he whispered in her right ear.

The sweet scent of his cologne wafted to her nose.

"Merry Christmas, darling," she said. "I thought I was going to spend Christmas alone again," she admitted.

"Not if I can help it," he said. "I want us to spend every Christmas together, if you want. And every holiday, and every day," he said with a sweet grin on his sexy lips.

Surprise and excitement rushed through her veins.

"Do you mean that?" she asked, not believing her ears.

"Only if you want to." He gave her a boyish grin.

"Of course." The feeling of joy leaped through her body. "I would *love* that," she said with a wide smile.

"When I said I love you last night in the shower, I meant it. It wasn't just sex talk."

Her heart melted with appreciation. She was glad she hadn't misread his words.

"I meant it too."

"You've always meant a lot to me. I enjoy being with you. I love being around you. And you know what? You're right. Life's too short to hold your feelings in and not let the people you care about know how you feel."

"I couldn't agree with you more." Her voice was soft and low.

"Thank you for the best Christmas present I've ever had," he said to her in a sensuous voice.

"Aww, same here, sweetie. You're the best gift I've ever had too."

She knew then and there, Chase's love for her was the gift that she would treasure every single day. This was the beginning of something very beautiful. And she couldn't wait to spend the holidays with Chase. She had a feeling this could be the beginning of another beautiful love story in the *Happily Ever After Cabin*.

Books by Ann Ric

Mountain Men of Charming Falls

Rescued by the Mountain Man (Evie & Jake)
Claimed by the Mountain Man (Candi & Erik)
Stranded with the Mountain Man (Lilly & Alex)
Christmas with the Mountain Man (Harmony & Chase)

Magic Protector Reverse Harem Trilogy

Magic Protector – A Steamy Paranormal Reverse Harem Romance (Book 1)
Magic Bound – A Steamy Paranormal Reverse Harem Romance (Book 2)
Magic Promise – A Steamy Paranormal Reverse Harem Romance (Book 3)

Mountain Men of Charming Falls

"Love makes the world go 'round"

Welcome to ***Mountain Men of Charming Falls***, the spicy instalove series based on a picturesque small mountain town by a lake that brings you closer to nature. A tranquil scenic escape from the busy city where residents in the cozy close-knit community look out for each other. Let the cool mountain breeze, clear night skies, beautiful romantic sunsets, and the fresh pine scents that fill the air bring you serene relaxation. Known for its camping sites, rustic cabin retreats, hiking trails, ski slopes, and yes, semi-recluse hot and sexy ex-military mountain men who live by the honor code: respect, loyalty, selfless service, integrity and courage in everything they do. Charming Falls is the perfect place to fall in love.

Rescued by the Mountain Man (Mountain Men of Charming Falls Book 1)

Rescued by the Mountain Man is a sweet & steamy short instalove romance novella featuring a gorgeous ex-military mountain man and a curvy woman.

Evie is a wedding planner-turned-jilted bride. She became a viral meme when she ran out of the chapel on her wedding day in tears. Why did she live-stream her wedding? Who was she to have it streamed? It wasn't like she was marrying a prince. She'd walked out of her wedding to her now ex-groom when a surprise guest showed up...

His wife!

Yep, that's right. She didn't know her now ex-groom was already married. So much for happily ever after. Humiliated and broken-hearted, she decides to go to a quaint small town where no one knows her; into the woods of the mountain town of Charming Falls to escape. To vanish. To disappear. Until she gets confronted by a bear…

Ex-military soldier and volunteer builder, Jake, wants to escape his past and live alone. Being a recluse in Charming Falls works for him…until a beautiful curvy woman shows up in distress. Will she be the one to break the protective barrier over his heart?

Bonus Chapter 1 – Rescued by the Mountain Man

"I need to get away. I need to clear my head," Evie said, tearfully, as she spoke to her friend over the speakerphone in her car while driving on the gravel road.

It was getting late now as she drove through the wooded area near the mountain to find her uncle's empty cabin. The road is somewhere off Cedar Lane. The name of the road is Second Chance Lane. Imagine that. Right now, she didn't think she was ever going to get a second chance at anything. Still, she was grateful for her uncle. He'd told her she could stay there for a while to heal her broken heart and escape the unwanted media frenzy. It was a few weeks before Christmas and this would be the worst Christmas ever.

It had been four weeks now since the now infamous wedding planner walked out on her own wedding before saying her vows as it was live streamed.

She was the laughing stock of social media now. Her business was now defunct in the worst possible way.

"That was so awful what happened to you, girl. I'm so sorry. You didn't deserve that."

"Thanks," Evie said, softly. "Who on earth told me it was a good idea to have my wedding live streamed for the world to watch? It wasn't like I was marrying a prince."

Her friend scuffed. "A prince? Please, the guy's a toad in *this* fairy tale."

On her wedding day, Evie's life, as she knew it, vanished before her eyes and in front of 50,000 followers.

Truth be told she never did feel right about her now ex and now she knew why. She should have followed her instincts and ran when he proposed to her. She should have followed her intuition.

"I've always been known as the overly cautious bore. A no-excitement chick."

"You?"

"Well, that's what my classmates used to call me all throughout high school and college. I always got my homework done early. I never went out to parties. Never smoked or tried any drugs. I was always the do-nothing play-it-safe girl." She sighed. "My dream this year was to do something spontaneous. Something bold. Something exciting that feels right to me. To follow my heart and not miss out. And I thought I could raise money doing it too. And now? It blew up in my face."

"It's not your fault," her friend tried to reassure her.

She had no choice but to walk out on her own live streamed wedding when a surprise guest showed up.

The surprise guest was John's *wife*!

Yep, the toad was already married and forgot to tell Evie. His wife lived in Europe and apparently heard what he was doing and flew over there.

Evie had the idea of live streaming her wedding for her ailing grandmother to see. Her grandmother couldn't leave the hospital so she thought it would be great for her to watch it as she had wanted to see her only grandchild get married.

Evie had also gathered sponsors for her wedding and had made enough to help cover her grandmother's monthly medical expenses. She'd also set up a fund to raise money for those suffering with dementia and mobility ailments. Something her dear grandmother had been diagnosed with and suffered with since her fall two years ago. Her wedding planning business was paying all the bills.

Now?

She was humiliated. Broken hearted. And soon, she'd be broke.

Now no one wanted to trust her with their wedding plans.

She was seen as a bad omen in the wedding industry. Damaged wedding goods.

Rejected so publicly at her own wedding.

That lying two-timer.

Could her life get any worse?

"I'm through with men," Evie declared over the phone as the tires of her car grinded over the gravel road.

"Aww, don't say that, Evie. Not all guys are lying scheming jerks like that creep."

"I know but right now, I'm not willing to give it another chance. Maybe love isn't for everyone."

Her heart sank.

Deep down she'd always wanted to be as happily married as her grandparents were—until her grandfather passed away last year. And she knew her grandmother wanted her to be happily married too.

She sighed deeply, feeling the weight of the world on her shoulders. She also wanted to give deserving brides their beautiful dream wedding and encourage them with their jittering nerves.

She even had a page on her blog titled "How to get over cold feet." She was supposed to be encouraging them that nothing could go wrong on their special day. How was she supposed to do that now?

They'd just seen what a disaster her wedding had been. Well, her almost-wedding.

She'd disabled the comments on her blog and social media page, opting to go silent indefinitely.

"Don't say that, girl. You just haven't met the right guy yet. And looks like your luck's about to change."

"Why do you say that?"

"Girl, don't you know about Charming Falls?"

"Yes, of course I do. It's a small mountain town where my uncle has a cabin. I've been here a few times, remember?"

Her heart fluttered in her chest when her mind slid to her uncle's hot and sexy neighbor, Jake. Her uncle once told her that Jake volunteered his time and helped build accessible homes for wounded and disabled vets and their families. And for those who'd lost their homes in storms in nearby towns. He'd do it for almost nothing. Just the cost of the supplies. He could make a killing but he didn't. He was a guy that just did the honorable thing to be of service in his community.

Would she see him again? She hoped she wouldn't see him in the state she was in now. She didn't want to see another guy again. But she couldn't stay in the city. She didn't want to be anywhere near WIFI either.

She was now in Charming Falls, the picturesque small mountain town on a lake that brought you closer to nature. The close-knit community full of locally-owned businesses and plenty of events kept the residents, tourists, nature lovers, hikers and photographers busy. The town's population of 7,000 year-round residents looked out for each other. It was also a tranquil scenic escape from the busy city life. She welcomed the cool mountain breeze and the fresh pine scents that filled the air reminding her of simpler times of her childhood when she went on camping trips.

A breath of fresh mountain air was what she needed. She needed to soak in the stunning mountain scenery and enjoy the mountain views.

The town had a cozy familiar feel to it with its beautiful landscapes and the best hiking trails around. Charming Falls High Street was the longest road that ran through the town with a breathtaking view of the mountains and the street was lined with a strip of quaint stores that included locally-owned bakeries with the scent of fresh pastries baked on site, a deli, locally-owned coffee shops with the tastiest freshly brewed coffee, giftshops, bookstores, delicious meals served in the tavern restaurants, chalets, the building supplies store, an art gallery, antique shops, bowling alley, yoga studios, the historic Charming Falls Inn, and of course the Charming Falls Cozy Bar & Grill that attracted many tourists.

Everybody loved visiting Charming Falls. And yes, the female visitors loved glancing at the hot mountain men who lived on the mountains in their rustic log cabins.

Many were ex-military men; war vets who worked in the town or volunteered their time helping out in the district while living off the land. Many still lived by their honor and protect code from their time in the military. And they were sexy as hell, so deliciously handsome they had the female tourists ogling their muscular fit bodies; the men spent most of their time doing physical work on the mountains and in their community.

Everyone knew each other in the town *and* each other's business. But she couldn't think about that right now. She just hoped they all didn't have WIFI and knew what went down on the Internet. Still, the residents all looked out for one another.

There were plenty of secluded log cabins on the mountains.

It was a perfect quiet escape with the most breathtaking views of nature. She needed that to clear the air. To clear her thoughts. To process her next move.

A person could easily get lost in the woods on the mountains if they weren't careful. There were so many small winding roads. Charming Falls had small-town charm with its pristine lakes and amazing mountains but man, did they have a lot of small winding dirt roads. The roads all looked the same.

Her friend chuckled. "Girl, you are in for a treat. Heard there's a lot of hot mountain men up there. And I mean so hot, the ice on the mountain could melt under their hotness. And they're all like honorable and shit like that. Most of them are ex-military soldiers. And *fit*."

Evie grinned and shook her head. "You've got to be kidding me. That's all you can think about is how hot and fit they are.?"

"Of course," her friend said, shamelessly. "Sometimes hot recluse ex-soldiers make the best lovers. It's raining mountain men, girl. You'd better leave your umbrella at home. That's the best way to get over your ex."

"Very funny. But I'm not into one-night stands." Evie playfully rolled her eyes. "Thanks for trying to cheer me up but I'm *really* through with men for now. Charming or not."

"You don't really mean that."

"Of course I do," Evie teased, shaking her head. "Thanks for being a good friend. But like I said, I'm on a break from men—even mountain men from Charming Falls."

"Just call me when you get there, hon," her friend said.

"Thanks, you're a solid friend," Evie said again. What would she do if she didn't have her friend to talk to right now. She felt so alone. So humiliated. So broken.

"Hey, no worries. And no more tears for that jerk, okay? He's not worth it. You're always there for everyone else. You need a break, girl. Who cares what anyone else thinks."

Unfortunately, I do.

No matter how much she told herself it didn't matter what others thought of her or her "sham business" as they now called it online, it *did* hurt. Words hurt her like a rock. She'd tried so hard to make it in the wedding planning business. She wanted to help deserving brides and grooms have a special day to remember. The irony was not lost on her that *she* was the one who would have a wedding day to remember—on the internet for the rest of her life!

61

Imagine a wedding planner having the most disastrous wedding in the history of weddings in that town. How could her business ever recover?

Image was everything and the image over the internet of her wedding day was anything but cool.

And her grandmother was so heartbroken over it too, which made it even worse.

Her business was over. She was now unemployed. The cancellations of her wedding planning services came in like a flood.

But nothing hurt more than John's betrayal.

What an idiot she had been to believe him.

What an idiot *he* was.

She'd made a list a long time ago about what she wanted in a man. He had to be:

> 1. *Sweet and sexy*
> 2. *Loves me for who I am*
> 3. *Passionate kisser*
> 4. *Great in bed*
> 5. *Makes my heart race, he takes my breath away*
> 6. *Strong and kind*

> 7. *Great in the kitchen, not just the bedroom*
> 8. *A great listener*
> 9. *Faithful and honest to the core*

She laughed at the thought now. Her ex was none of that. The last item on the list was so important too. Being faithful and honest. Her ex was a con artist. Plain and simple. A would-be bigamist. What did she ever see in him? Maybe she was expecting too much. If a guy couldn't be faithful to her, well, there was no way she'd stay with him.

After she ended her phone call with her friend, Evie narrowed her eyes, looking for her uncle's old cabin as she drove slowly on the dirt road.

Second Chance Lane must be around there somewhere.

Unfortunately, the exact location wasn't on the map, so she had to figure it out based on his instructions. Her uncle had left the state a while ago and was spending more time down south in the warmer weather. Her uncle had no children of his own and always treated her like a daughter.

Just then, she saw a creature run in front of her car and swerve so she wouldn't hit the little thing. Was it a squirrel or a beaver? She couldn't tell and didn't know if

63

these small animals even lived around that neck of the woods.

Unfortunately, her car swerved and took a nose dive into a ditch with a thump sound as it hit a tree.

"Oh, great. I'm in the ditch. Much like my career now," she whispered to herself, breathing hard, her heartbeat pounding in her chest.

She heard a horrible sound erupt from the engine. Her car wasn't exactly new but she loved old Tom. Yep, she named her car Tom. At least, *he* was reliable and never lied to her. He was there when she needed. And she took great care of him.

Unfortunately, this accident looked like it would be the straw that broke its back.

Evie surveyed her car when she got out. The front was totalled.

She reached into her phone and read the screen in horror.

No service.

Oh, great.

Her heart leaped with anxiety in her chest.

She was in an area of the mountains that had weak cell phone signal.

What a great spot to have your car break down, she thought with an air of sarcasm.

She was hoping to charge it once she reached the cabin but right now she didn't know *when* she'd reach it and she couldn't call her friend back to tell her she was stuck in the mountains. No one would find her or know what happened to her.

The sun was beginning to set.

Evie didn't have much time before dark. She had no idea just how far the cabin was from there but she had no choice but to walk to the nearest civilization. She knew it would be way too dangerous to stay there and hope someone spotted her.

The first rule of camping was to make sure you could get help—if needed. She'd heard that a signal mirror could be seen up to a hundred miles away. She would need some sort of survival reflective signal mirror to reflect the sunlight and alert any potential rescuers, or some sort of beacon to alert help.

But then again, what if she ended up alerting wild animals like bears or wolves instead of help?

Her heart thumped hard in her chest at the thought.

She was so screwed.

Okay, Evie, you'll be okay. Just keep walking. Your uncle's cabin can't be that far from here.

That's what she hoped. But as she took each step, her hope faded. All the small dirt roads looked the same around there. And without access to her GPS, she had no idea how close she was. The roads weren't even on the Google map.

"Ouch." She stepped on a broken tree branch and scraped her ankle. Now she was hobbling as she walked.

Man, she must look like quite a sight.

A chill came around her, then…

She heard a sound.

It was the type of sound that made the hairs on your skin stand up.

She heard a low growl from an animal and felt a presence as the cracking sound of someone or something stepping on tree branches on the ground could be heard. When she turned around, a large grizzly bear stood a few feet away from her.

Her breath caught in her throat. Panic swept over her spine.

Her instinct was to run but she'd heard it was best to stay calm.

Well, how on earth could she stay calm at a time like this?

Her eyes widened in terror.

Her pulse fired up.

She must have been shaking in her boots because the bear kept staring at her while inching closer.

**Thank you for reading this sample. Available now – the full novella "Rescued by the Mountain Man Book 1" by Ann Ric.

Claimed by the Mountain Man (Mountain Men of Charming Falls Book 2)

A sweet, grumpy ex-military mountain man and a shy, curvy wedding floral arranger. An undeniable chemistry. Can love bring them together?

When Candi, a talented floral designer who makes floral arrangements for lonely patients or deserving brides on a budget, finds herself lost on the mountains without cell phone service on her way to her friend's wedding, she knows she's in trouble…

Until she's rescued by a gorgeous mountain man with biceps of steel and a sweet, grumpy demeanor. Should she trust her heart around this handsome recluse?

Stranded with the Mountain Man (Mountain Men of Charming Falls Book 3)

After her boss, who is also her ex, leaves her at the company's camping trip site, Lilly finds herself stranded in the middle of a brewing storm…

Until she's rescued by a gorgeous, grumpy ex-military mountain man with the most breathtaking physique and stunning features she's ever seen. She's supposed to be on a break from dating, so why is she falling for this hero?

Christmas with the Mountain Man Mountain Men of Charming Falls Book 4)

After her now-ex broke off with her last Christmas, Harmony decided to never marry or celebrate the holidays...but her godmother had other plans. Harmony finds herself in Charming Falls to put up the Christmas tree in her godmother's *Happily Ever After* log cabin while she's away. But she soon runs into unexpected trouble in the form of a strikingly gorgeous mountain man.

Ex-military mountain man Chase wasn't looking for love, until love came to his door…his mother's friend asked him to put up the Christmas tree in her log cabin. But he wasn't expecting an intruder; a beautiful curvy woman…

*"Think of the things that make you happy,
not the things that make you sad…"*

- Robert E. Farley

Coming soon…

More sizzling short romance novellas in the Mountain Men of Charming Falls series by Ann Ric

ABOUT THE AUTHOR

Ann Ric enjoys writing steamy paranormal romance novels and sizzling hot contemporary romance short stories with a happily ever after. She loves to read romance novels featuring strong characters and breathtaking worlds. You can reach her by email at heartandsoulbooks7@gmail.com

Milton Keynes UK
Ingram Content Group UK Ltd.
UKHW041822131124
451149UK00001B/21